CW00848406

The Mystery of
Lydia Dustbin's Diamonds

Brough Girling and Tony Blundell

A & C Black · London

Best Friends · Jessy and the Long-short Dress ·
Jessy Runs Away · **Rachel Anderson**
Changing Charlie · Clogpots in Space · **Scoular Anderson**
Ernest the Heroic Lion-tamer · Ivana the Inventor · **Damon Burnard**
Weedy Me · **Sally Christie**
Something Old · **Ruth Craft**
Almost Goodbye Guzzler · Two Hoots · **Helen Cresswell**
Magic Mash · Nina's Machines · **Peter Firmin**
Shadows on the Barn · **Sarah Garland**
Clever Trevor · The Mystery of Lydia Dustbin's Diamonds · Nora Bone ·
Nora Bone and the Tooth Fairy · **Brough Girling**
Private Eye of New York · Sharon and Darren · **Nigel Gray**
The Thing-in-a-Box · The Thing-on-two-Legs · **Diana Hendry**
Desperate for a Dog · More Dog Trouble · Houdini Dog · **Rose Impey**
Georgie and the Computer Bugs · Georgie and the Dragon ·
Georgie and the Planet Raider · **Julia Jarman**
Cowardy Cowardy Cutlass · Cutlass Rules the Waves · Free With Every Pack ·
Mo and the Mummy Case · The Fizziness Business · **Robin Kingsland**
And Pigs Might Fly! · Albertine, Goose Queen · Jigger's Day Off ·
Martians at Mudpuddle Farm · Mossop's Last Chance · Mum's the Word ·
Michael Morpurgo
Granny Grimm's Gruesome Glasses · **Jenny Nimmo**
Grubble Trouble · **Hilda Offen**
Hiccup Harry · Harry Moves House · Harry's Party · Harry the Superhero ·
Harry with Spots On · **Chris Powling**
Grandad's Concrete Garden · **Shoo Rayner**
Rattle and Hum – Robot Detectives · **Frank Rodgers**
The Father Christmas Trap · **Margaret Stonborough**
Our Toilet's Haunted · **John Talbot**
Pesters of the West · **Lisa Taylor**
Jacko · Lost Property · Messages · Rhyming Russell · **Pat Thomson**
Monty, The Dog Who Wears Glasses · Monty Bites Back · Monty Ahoy! ·
Monty must be Magic! · Monty Up To His Neck in Trouble ·
Monty's Ups and Downs · **Colin West**
Ging Gang Goolie – It's An Alien ·
Stone the Crows, It's a Vacuum-cleaner · **Bob Wilson**

First published 1996 by A & C Black (Publishers) Ltd
35 Bedford Row, London WC1R 4JH

Text copyright © 1996 Brough Girling
Illustrations copyright © 1996 Tony Blundell
ISBN 0–7136–4426–5

A CIP catalogue record for this book
is available from the British Library.

Filmset by Kalligraphic Design Ltd, Horley, Surrey
Printed in Great Britain by William Clowes Ltd, Beccles, Suffolk

Chapter One

The mystery of Lady Lydia Dustbin's diamonds is one of the most mysterious mysteries of all time. It began one fine summer's day with the news that the Honourable Miss Lydia Teapot had secretly married Lord Charles De Grey Dustbin.

I now pronounce you man and wife — sorry, I mean Lord and Lady...

Lydia's friends were very surprised . . .

Miss Bunty Benenden

A secret wedding!
How romantic!!!

Mr Sheerluck Holmes

Hmmm . . .
a secret wedding!
How strange . . .

Old Clodpole the gardener

The old gal married!
Never thought
that 'ud 'appen!!

The main reason for their surprise,
however, was that while everyone
had heard of the Honourable Miss
Lydia Teapot, no one had ever heard
of Lord Charles De Grey Dustbin.

Not yet they haven't!

4

The reason that everyone had heard of Miss Lydia Teapot was that she was very rich. She had recently inherited everything from her father, Clarence, the last of the great Staffordshire Teapots.

THE TOMB OF THE TEAPOTS

She had even inherited the famous and very precious Teapot Diamonds.

I know that, stupid! The old bat's diamonds are worth an absolute fortune!

As the wedding had been a secret one, Lady Lydia suggested to her new husband that they should hold a party for all her poshest friends so that they could meet him.

After all Charles, you are so handsome and charming! I want to show you off to all my friends, and a party will be such fun!

Of course it will, my little scrummy-wummykins! My precious little honey-pie-toodle-pot!

Oh Charles, you're such an angel!

The daft old trout's not quite right about that!

Lady Lydia was so excited that she sent out the invitations straight away.

In celebration of their recent wedding, Lord Charles De Grey Dustbin & The very stately Lady Lydia Dustbin, invite

. . . .

to a slap-up house party next weekend.

Food, drinks, fox-hunting, shooting, fishing, games, dancing, and staying in bed on Sunday morning until quite late.

At their very stately home:
Teapot Towers,
Nether Regis-cum-Offit,
Staffordshire.

Oh no! Not fox-hunting!

Everyone she asked to the party thought that it was a splendid idea, especially as it gave them the chance to meet the mysterious Lord Dustbin.

Major Disaster for instance:

I say, old Lydia getting hitched at long last! And to a chappy I've never heard of! Most sportin' of her to ask me to a party. I'll take my shootin' togs and my guns and Trusty, my trusty foxhound.

Trusty the trusty fox hound

And Lydia's niece, Bunty Benenden, thought it sounded simply sooopa:

Young Freddie Gadabout-Town
replied to his invitation
immediately:

Dear Lady Lydia,
    I was mighty thrilled and no mistake
to get your jolly kind invitation. My life
is pretty full of parties at the moment, but
I'd love to buzz down to Teapot Towers at the
weekend. I'll be coming in my own aeroplane
on Saturday morning, so please get old
Clodpole your gardener chappy to clear a
landing strip for me on the flat land down
by the lake. Must fly – gosh, I've made a bit
of a joke! Yours
            Freddie Gadabout-Town.
P.S. I hope you'll be inviting a pretty young
girl or two. Mother says it's time I got
married too.

Mr Sheerluck Holmes, famous detective and bit of a know-all, was very pleased to be asked.

And Police Inspector Broom (of the Yard) wrote his reply on a page of his special police notebook:

As the replies came back Lady
Lydia ticked off the names on a list:

Major Disaster (& Trusty the trusty foxhound) ✓✓
Bunty Benenden ✓
Freddie Gadabout-Town ✓
Mr Sheerluck Holmes (& Dr Watson-Telly) ✓✓
Inspector Broom (of the Yard) ✓

Then she started making lists of
things she would need for the
party, and telephoned the village
shop to order jelly, and cakes and
lots of lemonade.

12

Finally, she made arrangements for young Freddie's aeroplane.

Chapter Two

By the following Friday afternoon everything was ready for the party of the century. There were

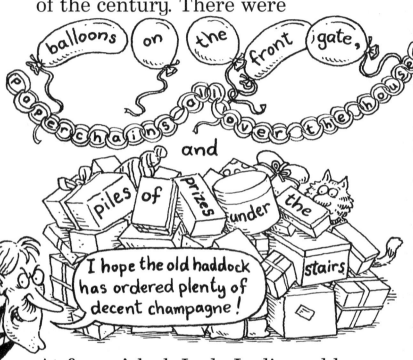

balloons on the front gate, paperchains all over the house and piles of prizes under the stairs

I hope the old haddock has ordered plenty of decent champagne!

At four o'clock Lady Lydia and her new husband went off to meet Major Disaster, Trusty the trusty foxhound and Bunty Benenden, who had all arrived at the local train station.

When they got back to Teapot Towers they all went into the library for a nice cup of tea and some homemade cakes, and discussed the coming weekend.

'I'm really looking forward to some shooting,' said Major Disaster. 'I like a party that goes with a bang!'

'And I'm looking forward to dancing the night away with a dashing young man!' said Bunty, excitedly.

'And I'm looking forward to having the most successful party in the world!' said Lydia.

And I'm looking forward to getting my hands on her diamonds, and getting out of here as fast as a rat up a drainpipe!

After tea, Police Inspector Broom
(of the Yard) arrived.

That evening, as everyone was changing into their best party clothes for a special candle-lit dinner, Lord Charles suggested to Lady Lydia that since this was such a special event, Lady Lydia should wear her special diamonds.

Lady Lydia rang for the butler.

Roland Butter had been the butler at Teapot Towers since before Lydia was born. He was the oldest and most trusted servant in the house.

The Teapot Diamonds were kept in a safe

Meanwhile, upstairs in her bedroom, Lady Lydia was ready for dinner.

Just as Lady Lydia and the other guests were sitting down for dinner there was a knock at the door . . .

25

Gasp, Holmes...!!   Quite so, Watson.   . . . .!!

Meanwhile, out in the grounds...

I say Minky, what a lovely set of sparklers!

Yes, they're the famous Teapot Diamonds.

This bird's a raven – a raven loony!

27

Later that evening, Sheerluck Holmes the famous detective asked all the guests to assemble in the drawing room. The famous detective looked seriously serious. 'We've found your butler, Lady Lydia,' said Holmes.

'Unfortunately he is dead, having received a blow on the back of the head from a blunt instrument — probably this bottle!'

'Gosh'

29

'I have to warn you all that everyone in this room is now under suspicion,' said Holmes firmly.

'Only Clodpole, the old gardener. I told him to clear a landing strip down by the lake,' replied Lady Lydia. 'And now I come to think of it, he had a bottle just like that in his jacket pocket!'

Chapter Three

The guests all went off to bed
rather early and without playing
any games. No one even suggested
a midnight feast. And the only
person who was up and about
bright and early the next day was
Clodpole the old gardener. He was
busy finishing the landing strip
down by the lake.

Coo-ah, this be 'ard work!

Golly gosh-look at
those lovely sparkly
old spectacles! They'll
brighten up my
nest even more!

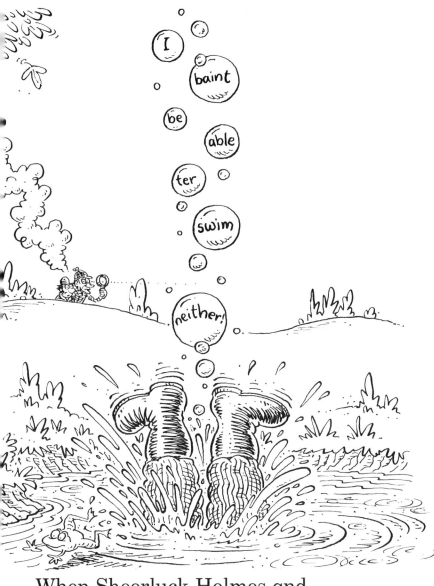

When Sheerluck Holmes and
Dr Watson-Telly arrived a few
moments later, the gardener was
nowhere to be seen.

CREEEK!!

Uh-oh!!

CRACKK!!

KKRUNCH!!

I say, what sheer bad luck, Holmes.
Shut up, Watson!
I say Holmes, why?
Elementary, Watson - because we've both been crushed to death!

Back at the house, Lady Lydia and her guests had got up and were having their breakfast in the magnificent dining room.

'I doubt it,' said Inspector Broom
(of the Yard).

These famous clever-dick London detectives aren't always what they're cracked up to be. But don't worry, your Lordship. I'm on the case! It's my belief that the butler chappy was not what he seemed...I'm working on the theory that he was part of an international diamond stealing gang. I suspect he has been killed by members of a second gang, who have now got the diamonds and are concealed in the house. They probably plan to sneak the jewels abroad, using a small private aeroplane...

Suddenly they heard the sound of a small private aeroplane. It was looping the loop.

The guests all agreed this was a good idea, and they went out on to the lawn.

43

Freddie landed his plane, and moments later joined the others on the front lawn.

'Good morning chaps,' he said.

Hey, I hope you don't mind me mentioning it, but as I was parking my plane I couldn't help noticing that the famous detective Sheerluck Holmes and his friend Dr Watson-Telly are lying under a tree by the lake, and the body of old Clodpole the gardener chappy is lying face-down in the water. Frightfully sorry and all that...

Poor Roland Butter was murdered yesterday. That's four people dead and it's only Saturday morning...
...and my diamonds are missing!!

'All right everybody,' said Inspector Broom sternly. 'There's more going on here than meets the ear! I shall take charge. Any more murders and I shall have to call the police!'

'I thought you were the police?' said Bunty, puzzled.

Yes, yes, sorry... I was forgetting. RIGHT! No one move! There's an international gang at work here and no mistake, and everyone is a suspect. I shall proceed on my bicycle to the area of the lake to comb it for clues which I shall write down in my special notebook. Stay here till I get back, and be prepared to answer some really tricky questions!

'It all sounds jolly suspicious to me!' said Major Disaster, his red face going even redder.

'I say . . .' said Bunty to young Freddie Gadabout-Town, 'the way you flew that aeroplane just now was so dashing and brave . . .'
'You really think so? Gosh,' said Freddie. 'Tell you what, why don't we go and start her up again, and I'll take you for a spin!'

Up in the sky above them, Raven decided that it was time to build a new nest. She used her new glasses to search for a nice safe place for it . . .

Major Disaster was soon running across the lawns of Teapot Towers, a loaded shotgun under each arm. Some distance behind him came Trusty his trusty foxhound.

Come on, Trusty. Keep up, or the murderer, whoever he is, will get away!

Whoooff! All right... all right... I'm coming!

Pant...!

Uh-oh!!

Ooops!

Still sleeping badger

Despite the gunsmoke, Trusty the foxhound soon spotted the diamonds.

Meanwhile, high in the mid-morning sky, Freddie was taking Bunty Benenden for a spin in his aeroplane . . .

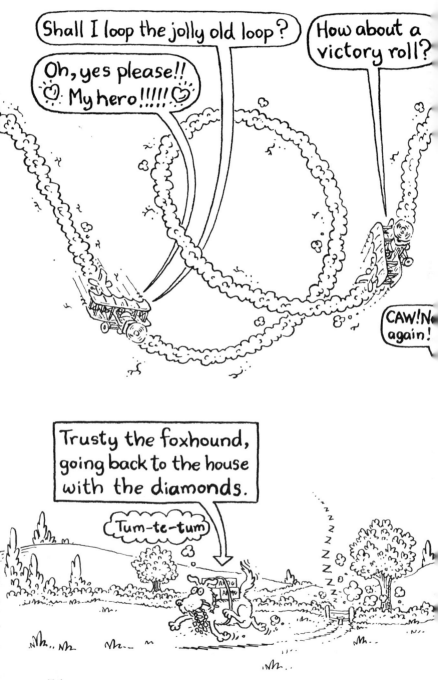

In Memoriam

Freddie Gadabout-Town
and
Miss Bunty Benenden

were never seen again.

~·Neither,·~

for that matter,

~·was·~

Police Inspector Broom

(of the Yard) . . .

Rest In Pieces

58

59

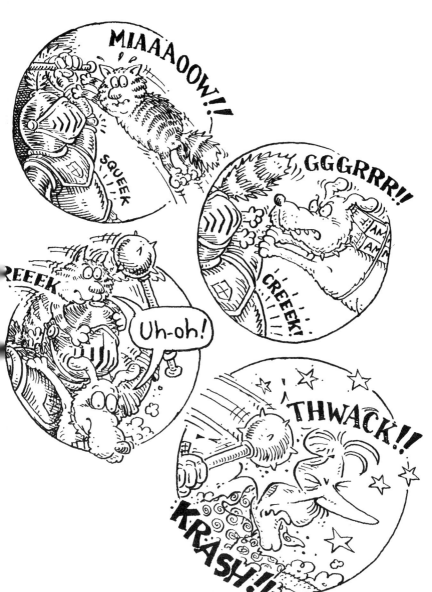

✳ This was the last thing
that the so-called Lord
De Grey Dustbin ever said.

. . . And what's this? A farewell note and a ticket to Monte Carlo. The cheat! The rotter! Oh silly me! How could I have been so stupid?
Although Lady Lydia Dustbin was very pleased to have her diamonds back, she was very upset that her party had not been a great success.
The worst thing about it is that I don't have any friends left to ask to my next party . . .
Dangerous mace!
Lots and lots of dust

THE END

To this day the disappearance and return of Lady Lydia Dustbin's diamonds remains a mystery, and no one can explain the strange accidents that spoilt her party.